This igloo book belongs to:

....

....

igloobooks

Published in 2015
by Igloo Books Ltd
Cottage Farm
Sywell
NN6 0BJ
www.igloobooks.com

HUN001 0215
2 4 6 8 10 9 7 5 3 1
ISBN 978-1-78343-656-9

Written by David Styring
Illustrated by Jo Byatt

Printed and manufactured in China

Catch Me If You Can!

David Styring

Jo Byatt

igloobooks

Once, there was a fish called Terence who was feeling very sad. He longed to swim just like his friends. He longed to impress his dad.

Ever since he could remember, Terence had only one wish,
To win the cup his dad had won and to be the fastest fish.

Terence was very determined.
He wanted to stand out.
He wanted to be good at swimming,
of that there was no doubt.

The problem for Terence was
that no matter how hard he tried,
Instead of swimming straight ahead,
he **waggled** from side to side.

The last race that Terence had entered, his dad sat in the crowd.
"This is a brilliant chance," thought Terence,
"to make my dad so proud."

Terence darted off with a splash! He dived further than the rest...

...but instead of going forwards, he just waggled east to west!

Soon, Terence was falling behind.

He had no chance of winning.

If Terence didn't speed up, he'd be back at the beginning!

Terence kept on swimming.

He wiggled his fins so fast.

He was sure he was going to win,

No thoughts of coming last.

Terence finally finished and listened for all the cheers.
He felt very upset indeed, when all he heard were jeers.

Dad swam over to Terence and said,
"Come on now, cheer up, son.
Don't take it all too seriously,
Swimming should be fun."

Something needed changing. It was plain for everyone to see.
Luckily, Dad had worked out what that simple change should be.
"You can do it, Terence," he said. "I know that you won't fail.
You just need to move your fins at the same time as your tail."

"When I was young," said Dad,
"I wasn't as fast as other fish.
Then I used my tail and fins together
and soon I got my wish."

So, Terence started practising, no matter what the weather.

Very soon his tail and fins worked perfectly together!

He listened to instruction, because he knew that Dad knew best.

Terence certainly put the work in.
His dad was SO impressed.

Race Day 1ST

On the day of the race, Terence said, "I will swim **SO** fast."
The other fish just laughed and cried out, "But Terence, you'll be last!"

"Get ready," said the swordfish. "On your marks, get set and GO!"

Terence darted away so fast, while all the rest were slow!

At one stage he was zigging left…

… next moment, zagging right.

Then he…

...jumped above the waterline...
...the most surprising sight!

Terence was like a torpedo…
… he shot over the line… he'd won!

The crowd all yelled and Dad shouted out,
"I'm SO proud of you, son!"

"Thank you, Dad," said Terence, "for always believing in me.
You always see the good things that nobody else can see."

Dad was very happy that his son was a swimming star.
"Never change," he said to Terence.
"We all love you just as you are."